MERCER MAYER'S
LC + THE CRITTER KIDS®

MY TEACHER IS A VAMPIRE

A Golden Book • New York

Western Publishing Company, Inc., Racine, Wisconsin 53404

A Mercer Mayer Ltd./J. R. Sansevere Book

Library of Congress Catalog Card Number: 93-73741
ISBN: 0-307-15957-4/ISBN: 0-307-65957-7 (lib. bdg.)   A MCMXCIV

Written by Erica Farber/J. R. Sansevere

LC

VELVET

LITTLE SISTER

TIGER

KOOL BEAR

SLICK RICK

SU SU   GABBY   TIMOTHY

GATOR   FLEX   HENRIETTA

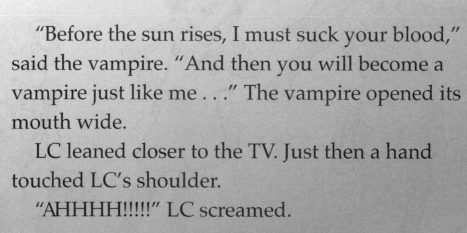

"Before the sun rises, I must suck your blood," said the vampire. "And then you will become a vampire just like me . . ." The vampire opened its mouth wide.

LC leaned closer to the TV. Just then a hand touched LC's shoulder.

"AHHHH!!!!!" LC screamed.

"You know you're not supposed to watch horror movies," Mrs. Critter said. She turned off the TV. "It's time for bed. You have a big day tomorrow. It's your first day of school."

LC was psyched to start school. His teacher was going to be Miss Candy. She was the best teacher in the whole school.

When LC got upstairs, he looked under his bed.
"What are you looking for?" asked Little Sister.
"Nothing," said LC.
"You're looking for vampires," said Little Sister,
"because of that movie."
"Am not," said LC.
"Are so," said Little Sister.

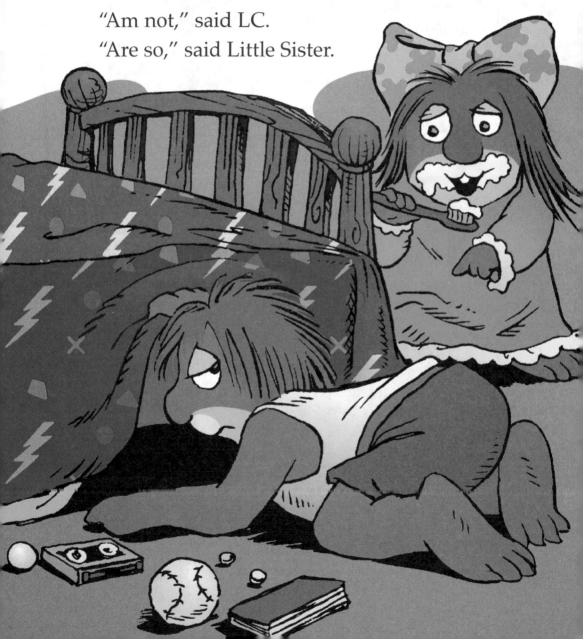

"Time for bed," said Mrs. Critter, walking into the room. "Good night, LC," she said.

"Good night, Mom," said LC.

LC's mom kissed him good night and turned off the light. As soon as she closed the door, LC turned the light back on.

LC couldn't wait for the sun to rise. He knew vampires didn't like the sun. That was his last thought before he fell fast asleep.

The next morning LC made breakfast.

"Dad, your eggs are ready," LC said.

Little Sister walked into the kitchen. "I'm not eating those eggs," she said. "They're burnt."

LC put half the eggs onto his plate and half onto his dad's plate. He thought they looked delicious.

"I'm going to have my favorite cereal," said Little Sister. She poured the cereal into her bowl. "*Count Dracul Duck Crunchies*, yum-yum."

LC looked at the cereal box. It had a picture of Count Dracul Duck on it. Vampires were for little kids, LC thought. He had nothing to worry about.

After breakfast LC and Little Sister started off
for school. Gabby was waiting by the mailbox.

"Did you see *Dawn of the Vampires* last night?"
Gabby asked.

"Yeah," LC said.

"I thought it was really scary," said Gabby.

"I wasn't scared," said LC.

"Oh, yeah," said Little Sister. "Then how come you slept with your light on?"

"I did, too," said Gabby. "And you know what? I bet there's a vampire right here in Critterville."

"There's no such thing as vampires," said LC. At least he hoped not.

LC and Gabby dropped Little Sister off at her classroom. Then they walked to Room Thirteen.

"Thirteen is bad luck," said Gabby. "We better keep our eyes peeled for vampires."

LC thought Gabby was being silly. He sat next to Tiger in the last row.

"Hey, dude," Tiger said. "How's it going?"

LC and Tiger slapped palms.

Gabby sat up front next to Timothy. He was the smartest kid in the class.

LC made a paper airplane. Then he threw it. LC watched the airplane fly up in the air. Just before it landed, everyone stopped talking. The airplane hit the floor right next to the biggest pair of shoes LC had ever seen.

A tall dark figure picked up the airplane very slowly. He looked at it carefully. Then suddenly he crumpled it in his hand and tossed it into the wastebasket.

"I'm Mr. Bat," the tall dark figure said. "I'm your substitute teacher."

No one said a word.

Mr. Bat looked into their eyes one by one. Then he closed the classroom door.

"Where did Miss Candy go?" asked Gabby. LC was wondering the exact same thing.

Mr. Bat didn't answer. He went over to the window and pulled down the shade. Then he walked over to Gabby's desk.

"No one knows where Miss Candy is," Mr. Bat said. "And no one knows when she'll be back."

LC was glad *he* hadn't asked that question. There was something very creepy about Mr. Bat.

Later that day LC, Gabby, Tiger, and Timothy were eating lunch together.

"I think Mr. Bat is a vampire," Gabby said. "Like the vampire in that movie *Dawn of the Vampires*."

"He is kinda strange," said Tiger.

"But just because he's strange doesn't mean he's a vampire," said LC.

Timothy looked up from the dictionary he was reading. "There are a number of ways to tell if someone is a vampire," said Timothy. "As a matter of fact, I think there's a comic book about vampires at the clubhouse."

"Why don't we go look for it after school?" asked Gabby.

"Okay," said LC. "But we have no proof that Mr. Bat is a vampire."

"And we have no proof that he's not a vampire," said Gabby. "Vampires can be very tricky, you know."

LC didn't say anything. All this talk about vampires was making him nervous.

After school LC and the Critter Kids went to the clubhouse. It was an old barn in LC's backyard. They climbed up to the loft where there was a big box of comics.

"I can't see," said Tiger.

"It's really dark up here," said Gabby.

"There's a flashlight downstairs," said LC. "I'll get it." LC went downstairs. He got the flashlight out of the cupboard. Then he quickly climbed back up the ladder.

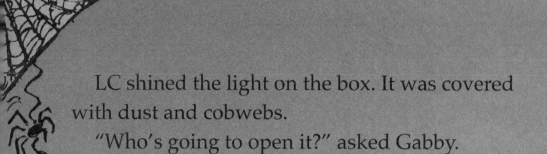

LC shined the light on the box. It was covered with dust and cobwebs.

"Who's going to open it?" asked Gabby.

"I will," said Tiger. He pulled the cover slowly off the box.

Timothy reached for the comic and read the first page out loud:

"*Vampires: How to Spot 'Em and How to Stop 'Em.*"
Just then there was a flash of lightning and a
crash of thunder. LC dropped the flashlight. And
everyone screamed.

"Don't worry," said Timothy. "It's just a storm."
But LC couldn't help it. He was worried.

The next day LC brought the comic to school. "Listen to this," said LC to Tiger. "'How to spot a bloodsucker in five easy steps.'"

Just then Mr. Bat walked into the room.

"'Number one: They like to wear black capes,'" said LC.

Tiger watched as Mr. Bat flung back his cape.

"'Number two: They hate sunlight,'" said LC.

Mr. Bat pulled down the window shade so only a tiny bit of sun got in.

"'Number three: They have fangs,'" said LC.

"Good morning, class," Mr. Bat said.

He opened his mouth very wide, revealing two large fangs.

LC and Tiger looked at each other. Maybe Gabby was right. Maybe Mr. Bat *was* a vampire.

As soon as the last bell rang, LC, Tiger, Gabby, and Timothy ran out to the schoolyard.

"I told you Mr. Bat was a vampire," said Gabby.

"Hold on," said LC. "We still have two more signs to check. We need a camera to take a picture of Mr. Bat."

"That's right," said Timothy. "Since vampires have no reflection, they will not appear in a picture. I have a camera in my briefcase. I'll take the picture."

"Now all we need is garlic," said LC.

"Right. All vampires are afraid of garlic," said Gabby. "We better get a lot of it."

"We'll meet you back here in half an hour," LC said to Timothy.

"Good luck, Timothy," they all said. Then they did the Critter Kid Shake.

Timothy headed up the school steps. He knew it was up to him. If he didn't get the picture, they'd never know for sure if Mr. Bat was a vampire.

Timothy heard something. Uh-oh, he thought, too late now. He held his breath and waited.

The door to the teachers' lounge creaked open. Someone coughed. Sweat broke out on the back of Timothy's neck. If he was caught, it would be the end. He had to get the picture . . . he just hoped he didn't get turned into a bloodsucker first.

Timothy ran to the bottom of the stairs. He peeked around the corner, and there was Mr. Bat. Timothy held up the camera and clicked. The flash went off and Timothy ran as fast as he could.

Meanwhile LC, Tiger, and
Gabby hurried into the supermarket. They
got a big cart.

"Where's the garlic?" Tiger asked.

"With the vegetables," said Gabby. "We need
every single piece of garlic there is."

They filled up their cart with garlic. Tiger even
stood on LC's shoulders to get the garlic strings.

"That comes to fifteen dollars and seven cents," said the checkout critter. "Must be some pizza you're making."

"We're not making pizza," said Gabby. "We're saving Critterville from vampires."

After they paid, LC, Gabby, and Tiger stuffed the garlic into their knapsacks. They put garlic strings around their necks. Then they headed back to school.

When LC, Tiger, and Gabby got to the schoolyard, Timothy was waiting for them. "Mr. Bat just left," he said. "We've got to follow him."

"First, put this on," said Gabby. She handed Timothy a garlic string. He put it around his neck.

Mr. Bat was just turning the corner when the Critter Kids caught up to him.

They followed Mr. Bat to the edge of town. There was nothing there but the Critterville Cemetery. Mr. Bat opened the iron gate and walked inside. LC, Tiger, Gabby, and Timothy all looked at each other. They had no choice. They had to go inside, too.

Mr. Bat walked to the middle of the cemetery. The Critter Kids tiptoed behind him. Suddenly Mr. Bat turned around. The Critter Kids ducked behind a big tomb. When they looked up, Mr. Bat had disappeared.

"I bet this is where he keeps his coffin," said Gabby. "I bet his whole vampire family is here, sleeping in their coffins."

LC shivered. He looked around the cemetery.

"We better get out of here," said LC. "Before the vampires rise out of their graves."

"There goes Mr. Bat!" Tiger yelled. "He's going out the back gate!"

The Critter Kids took off across the cemetery.

They followed Mr. Bat to an old house.
Suddenly the lights went on in the basement. The
Critter Kids all crept up to the basement window.
"I bet that's Miss Candy in there," said Gabby.
"I bet Mr. Bat is turning her into a vampire."
"What are we going to do?" asked Tiger.

Just then LC slipped. He knocked into the window with a loud bang. Mr. Bat looked up. He went over to a screen on the other side of the room. The Critter Kids watched in horror as Mr. Bat disappeared. A few seconds later, a big bat came flying toward them.

"Shape shifting!" screamed Timothy. "Watch out! Mr. Bat turned himself into a bat."

"Aahhh!!!" they all screamed and ran home as fast as they could.

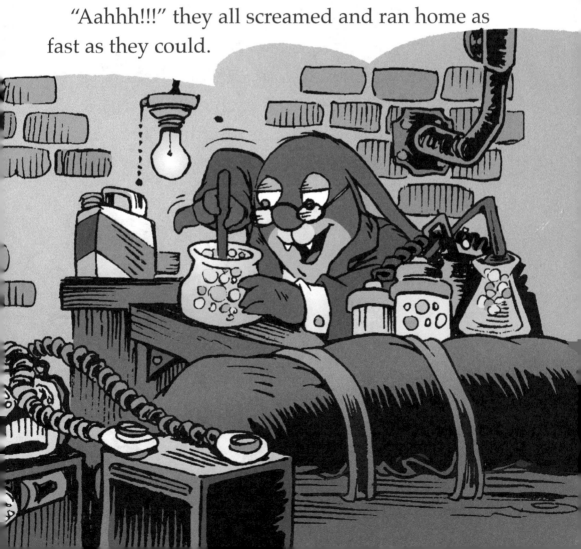

The next morning Gabby, LC, Tiger, and Timothy all wore their garlic necklaces to school. They carried their knapsacks full of garlic, too.

"Oooh, gross, you guys smell," said the other kids in their class.

"I know," said LC, "but we're saving Critterville."

"From what?" somebody asked.

"From him!" yelled LC.

Everybody turned to look. It was Mr. Bat.

"Don't worry. There's enough garlic here for everybody," Gabby said. She and the Critter Kids handed out the garlic.

Just then the bell rang. The Critter Kids marched down the hallway to Room Thirteen.

Gabby, Tiger, Timothy, and LC dumped the rest of the garlic onto Mr. Bat's desk.

Mr. Bat walked into the room. "I smell garlic," he said.

"That's right," said Gabby. "We're not going to let you turn us into vampires."

"Yeah," said LC. "We saw you turn into a bat last night."

"You shape shifter," said Timothy. "I bet you can turn into a smoky mist, too."

"And we know you live in the cemetery," said Tiger.

"Where's Miss Candy?" asked Gabby. "We know you've got her."

"You're right," said Mr. Bat. "She's right here."

Miss Candy walked into the room. "Sorry I missed the first day of school," she said. "I got married yesterday. But now I'm back. And Mr. Bat can return to his bat research."

Mr. Bat explained that he was doing bat research in his basement. And one of the bats had gotten loose. The reason that he kept pulling down the shade was because he had a headache. His fangs were new teeth he had gotten from the dentist. They were the wrong size. And he didn't live in the cemetery. It was just a shortcut to get to his house.

The Critter Kids all laughed. They had made a big mistake. "Sorry, Mr. Bat," they said.

Mr. Bat laughed. He thought it was funny, too.

The Critter Kids went to the clubhouse after
school. They put the vampire comic book back in
the box and closed the lid.

"I think we've all had enough of vampires,"
said LC.

Just then Little Sister walked in. "Here's your
picture," she said. "Mom picked it up for you."

"Picture?" said Gabby.

"Yeah," said LC. "Remember Timothy took that
picture of Mr. Bat to prove whether or not he was
a vampire."

"Yeah, if he wasn't in the picture, then he'd be a vampire," said Timothy. "Isn't that silly?"

"Yeah," said Tiger.

They all laughed.

Little Sister held up the picture. "How come you guys took a picture of an empty hallway?" she asked.

"What?!!" they all screamed.

Little Sister held up the picture. Mr. Bat was nowhere to be seen!